Patna
500 CE
Yangshuo
1600 CE
Canton
1860 CE

A Stone for Sascha

AARON BECKER

CANDLEWICK PRESS

for Lily & Minna

 First edition 2018. Library of Congress Catalog Card Number pending. ISBN 978-0-7636-6596-8. The illustrations were painted digitally on a tablet.
Candlewick Press, 99 Dover Street, Somerville, Massachusetts 02144. visit us at www.candlewick.com.
Printed in Humen, Dongguan, China. 18 19 20 21 22 23 APS 10 9 8 7 6 5 4 3 2 1

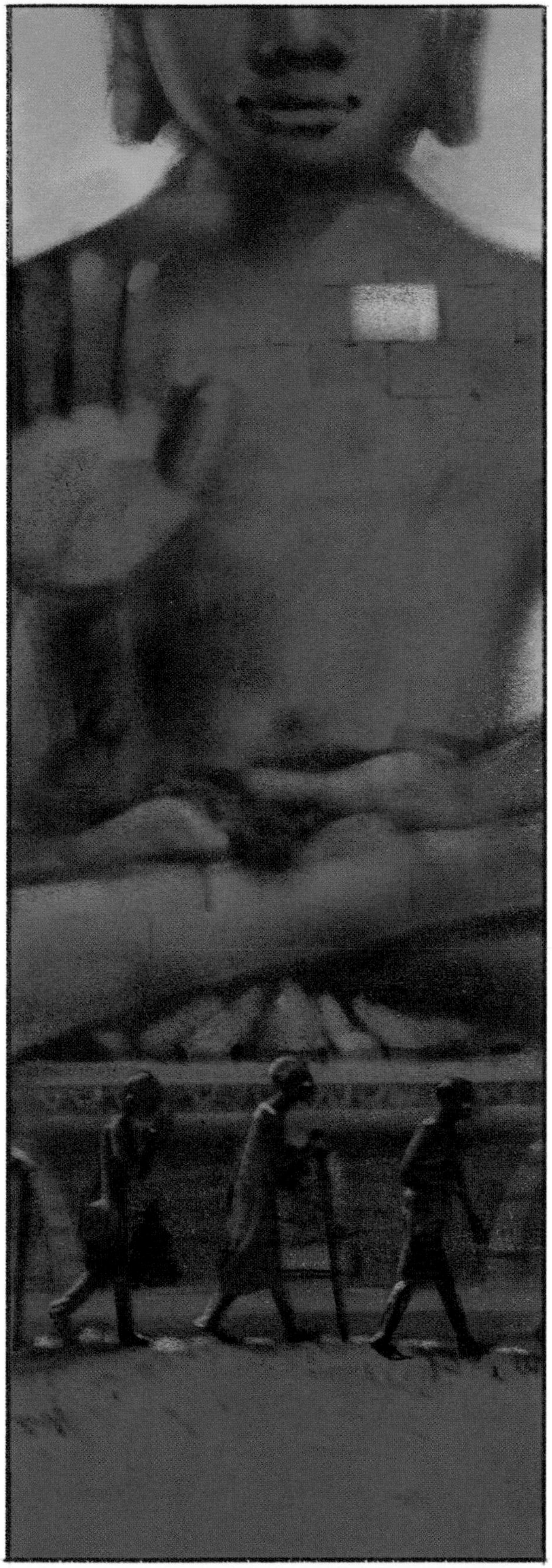
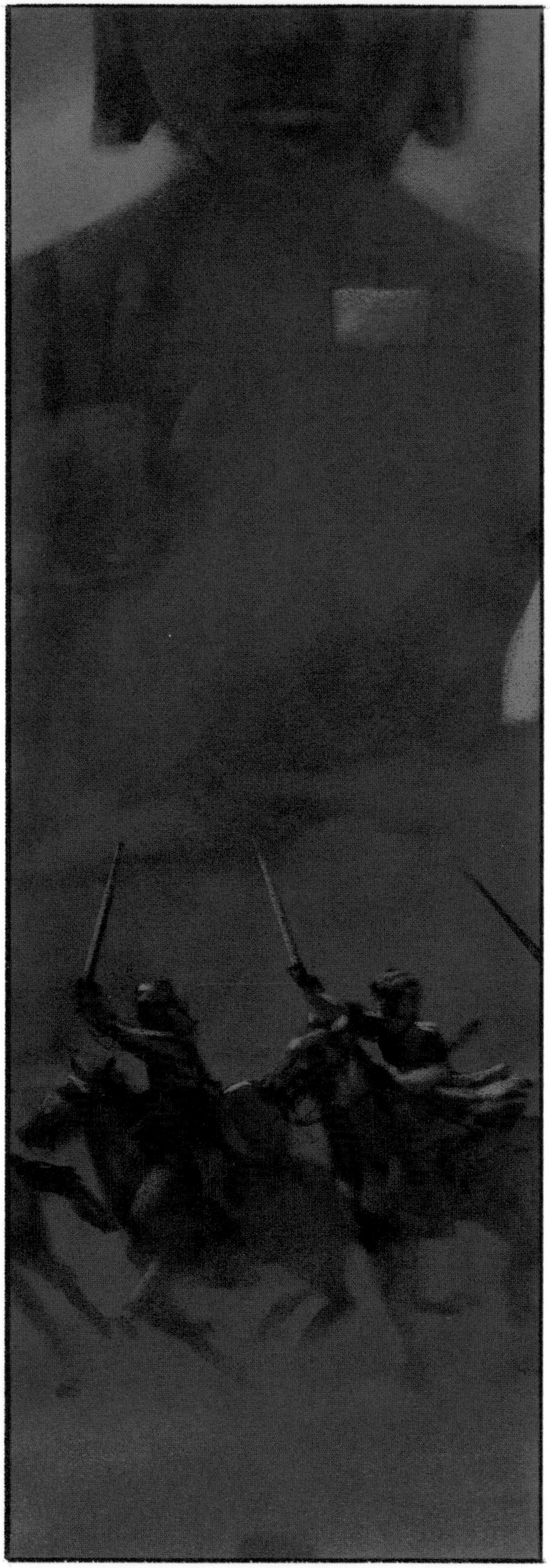
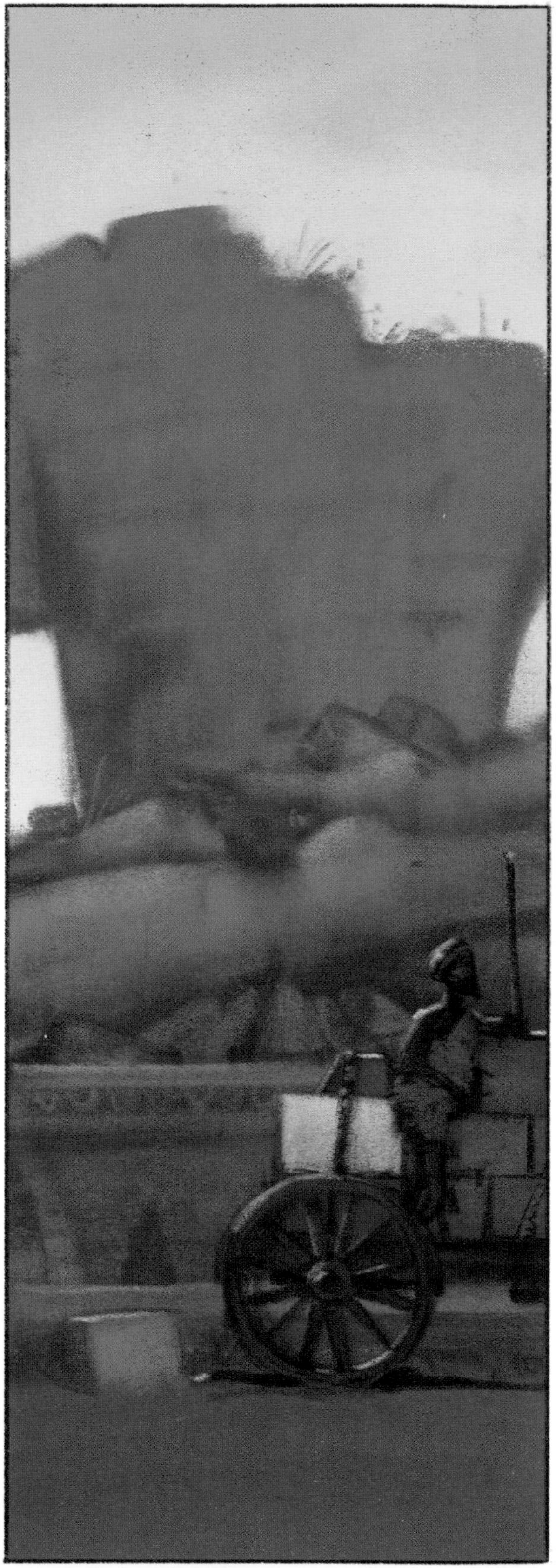

緣

Honolulu
1860 CE